'THE GARDEN GNOMES OF GRANTHA

1. PADDY PANTS DOWN

2. ARTHUR

3. GRUMPY MICK

4. ANDY'S SPACE ADVENTURE

5. LEG - A - LESS

6. HENRY'S NEAT & TIDY BUSH

7. LEAPING LEONARD

8. SEENO, HEARNO & SPEAKNO

9. THE WIZARD'S SLEEVE

10. GEOFF & DAVE'S SPORTING ANTICS

11. NANCY

12. THE NAUGHTY TRIPLETS

13. DARBY, TERRANCE & TRENT

14. THE THREE AMIGOS

Written by M F Katori 2020

Illustrated by M F Katori 2020

Paddy pulls his pants down,

he likes to show his bum.

He thinks that he is groovy,
he thinks that he is fun.

He showed it to the postman,
the postman wasn't impressed.

He glared at him and told him,

"Paddy please get dressed."

He showed it to the dustmen,

the dustmen thought him rude.

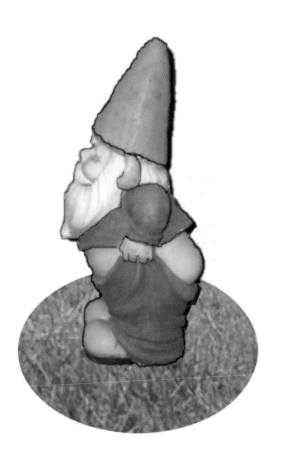

They shouted from
the window,

"PULL YOUR PANTS UP DUDE."

But Paddy thought it funny
to show off his bare behind.

So he kept on pulling his pants down,
he had that frame of mind.

He showed it to the gardeners' dog,

the Brigadier he did yap.

When the gardener turned around,

he pulled them up quick snap.

The gardener didn't like the noise,

he told the dog to "STOP."

He didn't see Paddy's pants down,

he didn't see them drop.

When the gardener wasn't looking,

down went Paddy's pants.

The gardener would spin around again and have a good old rant.

"STOP BARKING BRIGGY."

This went on and on all day,

'till the gardener saw his bottom.

"Paddy you're a naughty gnome,

pull your pants up that's just rotten."

But Paddy left them down,

he just wasn't going to be told.

So the gardener turned the hose on and gave it a good old scold.

The gnome's bum turned bright red,
he wasn't very happy.

That will stop the naughty gnome,
that will teach that Paddy.

COMING SOON

OTHER TITLES IN THE GRANTHAM MANOR SERIES :

'THE PIXIES OF GRANTHAM MANOR'

'THE FAIRIES OF GRANTHAM MANOR'

'THE WITCHES OF GRANTHAM MANOR'

ALSO AVAILABLE

'THE BEAUTIFUL ISLAND OF POWLEY'

"A fantastically humorous nonsense adventure" for 2yrs and up.

Did you ever wonder what happened to the owl and the pussycat? Well I am here to tell you, so settle down and prepare to sail away on a magical journey to the place where the bong trees grow in this enchanting tale based on Edward Lear's "The owl and the pussycat."

Intrigued?

M F Katori's spellbinding and delightful tale of wit and charm will leave your little ones dreaming of the sights they would see if they went to "The Beautiful Island of Powley."

For more information about my books, short stories, news and events etc, please visit my website and sign up to my mailing list.

https://maxinekatori.wixsite.com/mfkatori

Many thanks

Printed in Great Britain
by Amazon